CLASSICS
Illustrated®

Victor Hugo
LES MISERABLES

essay by
Sherwood Smith, M.A.

ACCLAIM BOOKS
STUDY GUIDE

Les Miserables

art by Norman Nodel

For Classics Illustrated Study Guides
computer recoloring by VanHook Studios
editor: Madeleine Robins
assistant editor: Gregg Sanderson
design: Scott Friedlander

Classics Illustrated: Les Miserables © Twin Circle Publishing Co.,
a division of Frawley Enterprises; licensed to First Classics, Inc.
All new material and compilation © 1997 by Acclaim Books, Inc.

Dale-Chall R.L. 7.1

ISBN 1-57840-017-1

Acclaim Books, New York, NY
Printed in the United States

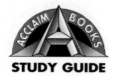

STUDY GUIDE

Les MISERABLES

VICTOR HUGO

THE UNFORTUNATE AND THE INFAMOUS ARE ASSOCIATED IN THE WORDS, LES MISERABLES. THERE WERE MANY SUCH PEOPLE IN FRANCE IN 1815. ONE OF THEM WAS JEAN VALJEAN.

AN HOUR BEFORE SUNSET ON AN EVENING IN THE BEGINNING OF OCTOBER, 1815, A MAN ENTERED A LITTLE TOWN OF D--.

HE WENT INTO THE MAYOR'S OFFICE, CAME OUT, AND TURNED HIS STEPS TOWARD AN INN.

WHAT WILL MON-SIEUR HAVE?

SOMETHING TO EAT, AND LODGING.

WHILE THE NEWCOMER WAS WARMING HIMSELF, THE INNKEEPER WROTE A LINE OR TWO ON A PAPER AND HANDED IT TO A CHILD.

TAKE THIS TO THE MAYOR'S OFFICE.

WHEN THE BOY CAME BACK WITH THE PAPER, THE HOST READ IT, THEN TOOK A STEP TOWARD THE TRAVELER.

MONSIEUR, I CANNOT RECEIVE YOU.

BUT I AM DYING WITH HUNGER! I HAVE WALKED SINCE SUNRISE. I WILL PAY!

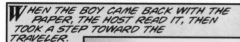

NO MORE OF THAT! I KNOW WHO YOU ARE. GO AWAY!

THE MAN BOWED HIS HEAD AND WENT OUT. HE WALKED AT RANDOM, SLINKING NEAR THE HOUSES. THEN HE ENTERED ANOTHER INN.

THERE IS THE FIRE; SUPPER IS COOKING IN THE POT. COME, WARM YOURSELF, COMRADE.

THE MAN SEATED HIMSELF NEAR THE FIREPLACE, HALF DEAD WITH FATIGUE. BUT A FISHERMAN WHO HAD BEEN AT THE FIRST INN BECKONED TO THE TAVERN KEEPER. THEY EXCHANGED A FEW WORDS, AND THE TAVERN KEEPER RETURNED TO THE TRAVELER.

YOU ARE GOING TO CLEAR OUT FROM HERE!

AH! YOU KNOW THEN.

THE MAN TOOK UP HIS STICK AND KNAPSACK, AND WENT OFF. HE TRIED SEVERAL HOUSES AND WAS TURNED AWAY. NIGHT CAME ON. EXHAUSTED, HE LAY DOWN ON A STONE BENCH.

IMPRIMERIE

JUST THEN AN OLD WOMAN CAME OUT OF THE CHURCH.

WHAT ARE YOU DOING THERE, MY FRIEND? YOU CANNOT PASS THE NIGHT SO.

I HAVE KNOCKED AT EVERY DOOR. EVERYBODY HAS DRIVEN ME AWAY.

THE OLD WOMAN POINTED TO A LITTLE, LOW HOUSE BESIDE THE BISHOP'S PALACE.

KNOCK THERE.

INSIDE THE HOUSE IN QUESTION LIVED THE BISHOP OF D--, A JUST, INTELLIGENT, HUMBLE, WORTHY, AND BENEVOLENT MAN. WITH HIM DWELT HIS SISTER AND HIS HOUSEKEEPER, MADAME MAGLOIRE.

I HAVE HEARD IN TOWN THAT THERE IS A DANGEROUS VAGABOND LURKING AROUND.

INDEED, MADAME MAGLOIRE?

YES, MONSEIGNEUR. THIS HOUSE IS NOT SAFE AT ALL, AND MONSEIGNEUR HAS THE HABIT OF ALWAYS SAYING, "COME IN," EVEN AT MIDNIGHT.

AT THAT MOMENT THERE WAS A VIOLENT KNOCK ON THE DOOR.

COME IN.

THE DOOR OPENED AND THE TRAVELER ENTERED, A ROUGH, TIRED, FIERCE LOOK IN HIS EYES.

SEE HERE! MY NAME IS JEAN VALJEAN. I AM A CONVICT. I HAVE BEEN NINETEEN YEARS IN THE GALLEYS. FOUR DAYS AGO I WAS SET FREE.

WHEN I REACHED THIS PLACE I WENT TO AN INN AND THEY SENT ME AWAY ON ACCOUNT OF MY YELLOW PASSPORT WHICH I HAD SHOWN AT THE MAYOR'S OFFICE, AS WAS NECESSARY. IT WAS THE SAME EVERY-WHERE. THEN A GOOD WOMAN SHOWED ME YOUR HOUSE. CAN I STAY?

MONSIEUR, SIT DOWN AND WARM YOURSELF. WE ARE GOING TO TAKE SUPPER PRESENTLY, AND YOUR BED WILL BE MADE READY WHILE YOU SUP.

YOU ARE GOOD PEOPLE!

*A*T THE BISHOP'S REQUEST, HIS SILVER PLATES AND CANDLESTICKS WERE PLACED UPON THE TABLE. IT WAS THE ONE LUXURY IN HIS GENTLE BUT AUSTERE HOUSEHOLD.

YOU TAKE ME INTO YOUR HOUSE. YOU LIGHT YOUR CANDLE FOR ME, AND I HAVEN'T HID FROM YOU WHERE I CAME FROM.

THIS IS NOT MY HOUSE, IT IS THE HOUSE OF CHRIST. WHATEVER IS HERE IS YOURS.

*A*FTER DINNER THE BISHOP LED JEAN VALJEAN TO THE ALCOVE WHERE HE WAS TO SLEEP. AS THEY WERE PASSING THE BISHOP'S ROOM, MADAME MAGLOIRE WAS PUTTING UP THE SILVER IN THE CUPBOARD.

*T*HE BISHOP LEFT HIS GUEST BEFORE A CLEAN, WHITE BED.

YOU LODGE ME IN YOUR HOUSE, AS NEAR TO YOU AS THIS! WHO TELLS YOU THAT I AM NOT A MURDERER?

GOD WILL TAKE CARE OF THAT.

JEAN VALJEAN WAS NOT A MURDERER. HE HAD BEEN A PRUNER AT FAVEROLLES, THE SOLE SUPPORT OF HIS WIDOWED SISTER AND HER SEVEN CHILDREN. ONE YEAR THERE WAS A VERY SEVERE WINTER. JEAN HAD NO WORK, THE FAMILY HAD NO BREAD.

WHAT SHALL WE DO?

THAT NIGHT, A BAKER IN FAVEROLLES WAS GOING TO BED WHEN HE HEARD A VIOLENT BLOW AGAINST THE BARRED WINDOW OF HIS SHOP. HE GOT DOWN IN TIME TO SEE AN ARM THRUST THROUGH THE OPENING. THE ARM SEIZED A LOAF OF BREAD.

THE BAKER PURSUED THE THIEF AND CAUGHT HIM. IT WAS JEAN VALJEAN.

JEAN VALJEAN WAS BROUGHT BEFORE THE TRIBUNALS AND FOUND GUILTY.

FIVE YEARS IN THE GALLEYS!

FOUR TIMES HE TRIED TO ESCAPE, AND EACH TIME HIS SENTENCE WAS EXTENDED. HE WAS SET AT LARGE AFTER NINETEEN YEARS AND, SULLEN AND HARDENED, HAD BEEN RECEIVED BY THE BISHOP.

A GOOD NIGHT'S REST TO YOU.

A FEW MINUTES AFTERWARD, ALL IN THE LITTLE HOUSE SLEPT. AS THE CATHEDRAL CLOCK STRUCK TWO, JEAN VALJEAN AWOKE.

THE SILVER PLATES IN THE CUPBOARD IN THE BISHOP'S CHAMBER WOULD BRING AT LEAST TWO HUNDRED FRANCS.

H IS MIND WAVERED A WHOLE HOUR. THEN HE ROSE TO HIS FEET, FUMBLED IN HIS KNAPSACK FOR AN IRON BAR, AND WITH STEALTHY STEPS MOVED TOWARD THE DOOR OF THE NEXT ROOM.

H E FOUND IT UNLATCHED. HE ADVANCED TO THE BISHOP'S BED AND STOOD LOOKING DOWN AT HIM WITH A STRANGE INDECISION.

S UDDENLY HE PASSED QUICKLY TO THE CUPBOARD. HE SAW THE BASKET OF SILVER AND TOOK IT.

H E CROSSED THE ROOM WITH HASTY STRIDE, TOOK HIS STICK AND KNAPSACK, STEPPED OUT OF THE WINDOW, RAN ACROSS THE GARDEN, LEAPED OVER THE WALL LIKE A TIGER, AND FLED.

THE NEXT DAY, THREE GENDARMES BROUGHT JEAN VALJEAN BACK TO THE BISHOP'S HOUSE.

AH, THERE YOU ARE! I AM GLAD TO SEE YOU. I GAVE YOU THE CANDLESTICKS, ALSO; WHY DID YOU NOT TAKE THEM ALONG WITH YOUR PLATES?

JEAN VALJEAN LOOKED AT THE BISHOP WITH AN EXPRESSION OF GRATITUDE WHICH NO HUMAN TONGUE COULD DESCRIBE.

THEN WHAT THIS MAN SAID WAS TRUE? WE MET HIM GOING LIKE A MAN WHO WAS RUNNING AWAY AND WE ARRESTED HIM. HE HAD THIS SILVER.

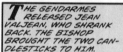

AND HE SAID IT HAD BEEN GIVEN HIM BY AN OLD PRIEST?

YES. IF THAT IS TRUE, WE CAN LET HIM GO.

THE GENDARMES RELEASED JEAN VALJEAN, WHO SHRANK BACK. THE BISHOP BROUGHT THE TWO CANDLESTICKS TO HIM.

MY FRIEND, BEFORE YOU GO AWAY, THERE ARE YOUR CANDLESTICKS. TAKE THEM.

JEAN VALJEAN, NEVER FORGET THAT YOU HAVE PROMISED ME TO USE THIS SILVER TO BECOME AN HONEST MAN. IT IS YOUR SOUL I AM BUYING FOR YOU. I WITHDRAW IT FROM DARK THOUGHTS AND I GIVE IT TO GOD!

JEAN VALJEAN FLED FROM THE CITY AS IF HE WERE ESCAPING. HE WANDERED IN THE COUNTRY ALL DAY, CONFUSED BY A MULTITUDE OF NEW SENSATIONS. HE WAS SEATED BEHIND A THICKET WHEN HE SAW A BOY COMING ALONG A PATH.

THE BOY STOPPED BY THE SIDE OF THE THICKET, WITHOUT SEEING JEAN VALJEAN, AND TOSSED UP SOME PIECES OF MONEY THAT HE HAD IN HIS HAND.

A FORTY-SOUS PIECE ESCAPED HIM AND ROLLED TOWARD THE THICKET NEAR JEAN VALJEAN. JEAN VALJEAN PUT HIS FOOT UPON IT.

MONSIEUR, MY MONEY

JEAN VALJEAN DID NOT APPEAR TO UNDERSTAND. THE BOY TOOK HIM BY THE COLLAR OF HIS BLOUSE AND SHOOK HIM.

I WANT MY MONEY! WILL YOU TAKE AWAY YOUR FOOT?

GET OUT!

JEAN VALJEAN ROSE TO HIS FEET, AND THE BOY TOOK TO FLIGHT. ALL AT ONCE JEAN VALJEAN SAW THE FORTY-SOUS PIECE.

WHAT IS THAT?

AFTER A FEW MINUTES HE SEIZED IT AND BEGAN TO WALK RAPIDLY IN THE DIRECTION IN WHICH THE CHILD HAD GONE. HE SAW NOTHING. THEN HE FELL UPON A GREAT STONE, HIS HEART SWELLED, AND HIS BURST INTO TEARS.

HOW LONG DID HE WEEP THUS? WHAT DID HE DO AFTER WEEPING? NOBODY EVER KNEW. BUT ABOUT THAT TIME A STRANGER ENTERED THE LITTLE CITY OF M - - SUR M - - ON THE VERY DAY THAT A GREAT FIRE BROKE OUT IN THE TOWN HOUSE.

THE MAN RUSHED INTO THE FIRE AND SAVED, AT THE PERIL OF HIS LIFE, TWO CHIDREN WHO PROVED TO BE THOSE OF THE CAPTAIN OF THE GENDARMERIE.

WHAT IS YOUR NAME, GOOD SIR?

FATHER MADELEINE.

IN THE HURRY AND GRATITUDE OF THE MOMENT, NO ONE THOUGHT TO ASK HIM FOR HIS PASSPORT. HE ESTABLISHED HIMSELF IN THE CITY AND INVENTED A PROCESS IN THE MANUFACTURE OF JET AND BLACK GLASS WARE. IN LESS THAN THREE YEARS, HE HAD BECOME RICH, AND HAD MADE ALL AROUND HIM RICH.

THERE IS FATHER MADELEINE'S FACTORY. AND THERE ARE THE NEW SCHOOLS AND HOSPITALS HE BUILT FOR THE POOR.

FIVE YEARS AFTER HIS ARRIVAL, THE SERVICES HE HAD RENDERED TO THE REGION WERE SO BRILLIANT THAT THE KING APPOINTED HIM MAYOR. HE REFUSED, BUT THE PEOPLE BEGGED HIM TO ACCEPT.

A GOOD MAYOR IS A GOOD THING. ARE YOU AFRAID OF THE GOOD YOU CAN DO?

So he became Monsieur the Mayor, honored and adored by all. One man alone held himself clear of this admiration. His name was Javert, and he was one of the police.

WHO IS THIS MAN? I AM SURE I HAVE SEEN HIM SOMEWHERE.

One morning, Monsieur Madeleine was walking along when he heard shouting. He went to the spot.

IT IS FATHER FAUCHELEVENT! HE HAS FALLEN UNDER HIS CART!

The whole weight of the cart rested upon the old man's breast.

WE HAVE SENT FOR A JACK. IT WILL BE HERE IN A QUARTER OF AN HOUR.

WE CANNOT WAIT. DON'T YOU SEE THE WAGON IS SINKING ALL THE WHILE?

LISTEN, THERE IS ROOM ENOUGH UNDER THE WAGON FOR A MAN TO CRAWL IN AND LIFT IT WITH HIS BACK. IS THERE NOBODY HERE WHO HAS THE COURAGE AND STRENGTH?

Nobody stirred. Then Javert came up.

I HAVE KNOWN BUT ONE MAN CAPABLE OF RAISING A WAGON ON HIS BACK. HE WAS A CONVICT IN THE GALLEYS AT TOULON.

MONSIEUR MADELEINE BECAME PALE. MEANWHILE, THE CART WAS SLOWLY SETTLING IN THE MUD.

MY RIBS ARE BREAK- ING! A JACK! ANYTHING!

MONSIEUR MADELEINE MET THE FAL- CON EYE OF JAVERT AND SMILED SADLY. THEN HE FELL ON HIS KNEES AND SLID UNDER THE CART.

THE BYSTANDERS HELD THEIR BREATHS. ALL AT ONCE THE ENORMOUS MASS ROSE.

HELP ME!

THEY ALL RUSHED TO THE WORK. THE CART WAS LIFTED. OLD FAUCHELEVENT WAS SAFE.

MONSIEUR MADELEINE AROSE. HE WAS VERY PALE AND COVERED WITH MUD, BUT HE LOOKED WITH A TRANQUIL EYE UPON JAVERT, WHO WAS STILL WATCHING HIM.

FAUCHELEVENT HAD INJURED HIS KNEE. WHEN HE WAS WELL, MONSIEUR MADELEINE GOT HIM A PLACE AS GARDENER AT A CONVENT IN PARIS. ANOTHER PERSON HELPED BY MONSIEUR MADELEINE WAS A YOUNG WOMAN NAMED FANTINE.

I MUST HAVE WORK!

COME IN. MONSIEUR MADELEINE HAS ORDERED THAT ANY HONEST PERSON MAY FIND WORK AND WAGES HERE.

ONE DAY, HOWEVER, THE OVERSEER OF THE WORKSHOP TOLD FANTINE THAT SHE WAS NO LONGER WANTED IN THE SHOP.

BUT WHAT WILL I DO? WHERE WILL I GO?

FANTINE'S LIFE BECAME VERY MISERABLE. NOBODY WANTED HER.

I DO NOT MIND SO MUCH FOR MYSELF. BUT I HAVE A CHILD WHO IS LIVING WITH SOME PEOPLE NAMED THENARDIER, IN MONTFERMEIL. I CAN NO LONGER SEND THEM ENOUGH MONEY TO CARE FOR HER.

THE MORE ALL BECAME GLOOMY AROUND HER, THE MORE FANTINE WORSHIPPED HER CHILD.

OH, TO HAVE COSETTE WITH ME! BUT I CANNOT BRING HER HERE TO SHARE MY MISERY.

ONE DAY FANTINE WAS INVOLVED IN A STREET FIGHT. SHE WAS TAKEN TO THE BUREAU OF POLICE BY JAVERT.

CARRY THIS GIRL TO JAIL. SHE IS IN FOR SIX MONTHS.

SIX MONTHS! BUT WHAT WILL BECOME OF MY DAUGHTER? I MUST PAY THE THENARDIERS, OR ELSE THEY WILL TURN AWAY MY LITTLE ONE.

JAVERT TURNED HIS BACK, AND THE SOLDIERS SEIZED HER BY THE ARMS. THEN A MAN WHO HAD ENTERED A FEW MINUTES BEFORE STEPPED FORWARD.

INSPECTOR JAVERT, SET THIS WOMAN AT LIBERTY.

BUT MONSIEUR THE MAYOR --

FANTINE SPRANG AT MONSIEUR MADELEINE.

YOU ARE THE MAYOR? WHY, YOU ARE THE CAUSE OF ALL THIS! YOU TURNED ME AWAY FROM YOUR WORKSHOP! THEN I COULD NOT EARN ENOUGH, AND ALL THIS WRETCHEDNESS CAME.

I KNEW NOTHING OF WHAT YOU HAVE SAID. WHY DID YOU NOT COME TO ME? BUT NOW, I WILL HAVE YOUR CHILD COME TO YOU, AND I WILL GIVE YOU ALL THE MONEY YOU NEED.

Monsieur Madeleine had Fantine taken to the infirmary, for she was very ill. He wrote to the Thenardiers directing them to bring Cosette at once, but they delayed. Meanwhile, a serious matter intervened.

WELL, WHAT IS IT, JAVERT?

SOME WEEKS AGO I WROTE TO THE POLICE IN PARIS AND DENOUNCED YOU AS A FORMER CONVICT NAMED JEAN VALJEAN. I SAW HIM TWENTY YEARS AGO WHEN I WAS ADJUTANT OF THE GALLEY AT TOULON. AFTER LEAVING THE GALLEYS THIS VALJEAN ROBBED A LITTLE BOY.

AND WHAT ANSWER DID YOU GET TO YOUR LETTER?

THAT I WAS CRAZY. THE REAL JEAN VALJEAN HAS BEEN FOUND. HE IS A SIMPLE SORT OF FELLOW WHO WAS ARRESTED FOR STEALING APPLES.

IN THE PRISON, A CONVICT SAW HIM AND CRIED OUT THAT HE WAS JEAN VALJEAN, WHO HAD BEEN WITH HIM IN THE GALLEYS. THEFT, FOR A CONVICT, IS NOT A FEW DAYS IMPRISONMENT, BUT THE GALLEYS FOR LIFE.

WHAT DID THE MAN SAY.

HE PRETENDS NOT TO UNDERSTAND. THE RASCAL IS CUNNING, BUT HE WILL BE CONDEMNED. THE CASE IS TO BE TRIED TOMORROW IN ARRAS.

YOUR PARDON, MONSIEUR, FOR SUSPECTING YOU. I OUGHT TO BE DISMISSED.

JAVERT, YOU ARE A MAN OF HONOR. I DESIRE YOU TO KEEP YOUR PLACE.

MONSIEUR MADELEINE WENT HOME AND PASSED THE NIGHT IN A TORMENT OF INDECISION. AT FIVE O'CLOCK IN THE MORNING HE STARTED FOR ARRAS. IT WAS NEARLY EIGHT IN THE EVENING WHEN HE ARRIVED.

MONSIEUR, WHERE IS THE COURT HOUSE?

DO YOU SEE THOSE FOUR LIGHTED WINDOWS? THEY ARE HAVING AN EVENING SESSION.

MONSIEUR MADELEINE ENTERED THE BUILDING AND FOUND HIMSELF BEFORE A DOOR. HE SEIZED THE KNOB CONVULSIVELY - - THE DOOR OPENED. HE WAS IN THE COURT ROOM.

HIS EYES WENT TOWARD A MAN SITTING BETWEEN TWO GENDARMES.

YES, HE RESEMBLES ME. GREAT GOD! SHALL I AGAIN COME TO THIS?

THE TIME HAD COME FOR CLOSING THE CASE. IT WAS EVIDENT THAT THE MAN WAS LOST. MONSIEUR MADELEINE ROSE.

GENTLEMEN, RELEASE THE ACCUSED. HE IS NOT THE MAN WHOM YOU SEEK, IT IS I. I AM JEAN VALJEAN.

I HAVE MANY THINGS TO DO. THE PROSECUTING ATTORNEY MAY HAVE ME ARRESTED WHEN HE CHOOSES.

HE WENT OUT AND RETURNED HOME. JAVERT CAME FOR HIM AS HE WAS VISITING FANTINE, WHO WAS NOW EXTREMELY ILL.

HURRY ALONG.

JAVERT SEIZED HIM BY THE COLLAR.

MONSIEUR THE MAYOR!

THERE IS NO MONSIEUR THE MAYOR HERE ANY LONGER.

JEAN VALJEAN TURNED TO JAVERT AND SPOKE RAPIDLY IN A LOW TONE.

GIVE ME THREE DAYS TO GO FOR THE CHILD OF THIS UNHAPPY WOMAN! YOU SHALL ACCOMPANY ME IF YOU LIKE.

THREE DAYS! ARE YOU MAKING FUN OF ME? I DID NOT THINK YOU SO STUPID!

MY CHILD! I WANT MY CHILD! MONSIEUR MADELEINE!

I TELL YOU THERE IS NO MONSIEUR MADELEINE! THERE IS A CONVICT CALLED JEAN VALJEAN, AND I HAVE GOT HIM!

FANTINE STARTED UPRIGHT, THEN SANK SUDDENLY BACK UPON THE PILLOW. SHE WAS DEAD. JEAN VALJEAN TURNED TO JAVERT.

NOW, I AM AT YOUR DISPOSAL.

JAVERT PUT JEAN VALJEAN IN THE CITY PRISON, BUT HE BROKE A BAR FROM A WINDOW AND ESCAPED. IN THREE OR FOUR DAYS HE WAS RETAKEN, BUT NOT BEFORE HE HAD WITHDRAWN SIX FOR SEVEN THOUSAND FRANCS FROM HIS BANKERS, AND CONCEALED THEM. HE WAS TRIED FOR ROBBING THE BOY'S COIN AND SENTENCED TO THE GALLEYS FOR LIFE.

IN OCTOBER, 1823, HE WAS SERVING ON THE SHIP ORION WHEN AN ACCIDENT OCCURRED.

THE TOPMAN HAS FALLEN FROM THE YARD!

SUDDENLY A MAN WAS DICOVERED CLAMBERING UP THE RIGGING. IT WAS JEAN VALJEAN.

IN A TWINKLING HE WAS UPON THE YARD. HE WAS SEEN TO RUN ALONG IT AND THEN LET HIMSELF DOWN ON A ROPE HE HAD BROUGHT WITH HIM.

HE SEIZED THE SEA- MAN AND HAULED HIM UP. LIFTING HIM IN HIS ARMS, HE CARRIED HIM TO THE ROUNDTOP, WHERE HE LEFT HIM IN THE HANDS OF HIS MESS-MATES.

THEN HE SLIDE DOWN THE RIGGING AND STARTED TO RUN ALONG A LOWER YARD. SUDDENLY, THE THRONG UTTERED A THRILLING OUTCRY - - THE CONVICT HAD FALLEN INTO THE SEA.

He did not rise to the surface, and it was believed he had been caught under the piles at the pier-head and drowned. However, Christmas Day found him in Montfermeil at the Thenardier Tavern.

AH, COSETTE! THAT IS THE WAY YOU WORK! I'LL MAKE YOU WORK WITH A COWHIDE!

THE CHILD IS YOURS, MADAME THENARDIER?

NO, MONSIEUR. SHE IS A LITTLE PAUPER THAT WE HAVE TAKEN IN THROUGH CHARITY.

SUPPOSE YOU WERE RELIEVED OF HER?

COSETTE? AH, MON-SIEUR, TAKE HER! WE GET NOTHING FROM HER MOTHER. WE THINK SHE MUST BE DEAD.

At that moment, Thenardier advanced into the middle of the room.

I MUST HAVE FIFTEEN HUN-DRED FRANCS FOR THAT CHILD.

VERY WELL. BRING COSETTE.

And a while later, Jean Valjean led the little girl, Fantine's child, along the road to Paris.

THEY ENTERED PARIS AT NIGHTFALL, AND WENT TO AN OLD BUILDING IN A LONELY PART OF THE CITY.

MUST I SWEEP?

PLAY!

WEEKS ROLLED BY. COSETTE BEGAN TO LOVE HER KIND OLD FRIEND, AND ALL OF JEAN VALJEAN'S AFFECTION WAS ATTRACTED TOWARD THE CHILD. THEN ONE NIGHT HE HEARD SOMEONE COMING UP THE STAIRS.

GO TO BED. LIE DOWN VERY QUIETLY.

HE PLACED HIS EYE TO THE KEYHOLE AND SAW A MAN PASS BY. IT WAS JAVERT.

HE IS STILL ON MY TRAIL!

LATER, JEAN VALJEAN WENT TO THE STREET DOOR AND LOOKED CAREFULLY UP AND DOWN. HE WENT UPSTAIRS AGAIN.

COME.

THEY BOTH WENT OUT. JEAN VALJEAN BEGAN TO THREAD THE STREETS, MAKING AS MANY TURNS AS HE COULD.

As eleven o'clock struck he turned his head and saw four men. He recognized Javert perfectly.

He doubled his pace, carrying Cosette. Finally he turned into an alley. The end of it was a great white wall.

I can scale the wall, but it would be impossible to carry Cosette.

His despairing gaze encountered the lamp post and the rope which raised and lowered the lamp. He cut it off and tied it around Cosette.

Taking the other end in this teeth, he began to climb. Half a minute had not passed before he was on his knees on the wall.

Before Cosette had time to think, she too was at the top of the wall. Jean Valjean put her on his back, crawled to a building with a sloping roof, slid down the roof, and jumped to the ground.

*H*E FOUND HIMSELF IN A SORT OF GARDEN. HE TOOK COSETTE INTO A SHED AND WRAPPED HER IN HIS COAT. SHE FELL ASLEEP. SUDDENLY A NOISE MADE HIM TURN.

THERE IS A MAN WALKING IN THE GARDEN!

*H*E TOUCHED COSETTE'S HANDS. THEY WERE ICY. HE SHOOK HER. SHE DID NOT WAKE.

I MUST GET HER IN A BED AND BEFORE A FIRE!

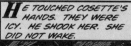

*H*E WALKED STRAIGHT TO THE MAN IN THE GARDEN.

A HUNDRED FRANCS FOR YOU IF YOU WILL GIVE ME REFUGE TONIGHT.

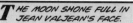

*T*HE MOON SHONE FULL IN JEAN VALJEAN'S FACE.

WHY, IT IS MONSIEUR MADELEINE! HOW DID YOU COME HERE? DID YOU FALL FROM THE SKY?

WHO ARE YOU? WHAT IS THIS HOUSE?

I AM FATHER FAUCHELEVENT. YOU LIFTED THE CART OFF ME AND YOU GOT ME A PLACE AS GARDENER AT THIS CONVENT. YOU SAVED MY LIFE.

WELL, YOU CAN NOW DO FOR ME WHAT I ONCE DID FOR YOU.

IN A HALF HOUR COSETTE HAD AGAIN BECOME ROSY BEFORE A GOOD FIRE. FOR FIVE YEARS THEY STAYED AT THE CONVENT. JEAN VALJEAN WORKED AS A GARDENER AND COSETTE WAS EDUCATED BY THE NUNS.

FINALLY THEY LEFT THE CONVENT AND WENT TO LIVE IN A SMALL HOUSE ON A DESERTED STREET. OFTEN THEY WALKED IN THE LUXEMBOURG, WHERE COSETTE, NOW BEAUTIFUL, ATTRACTED THE ATTENTION OF A POOR YOUNG LAWYER NAMED MARIUS PONTMERCY.

OH, SHE IS VERY PRETTY.

ONE DAY COSETTE RAIISED HER EYES. THEIR GLANCES MET. FROM THAT DAY ONWARD, THEY ADORED EACH OTHER.

MARIUS FOLLOWED COSETTE HOME. HE SPOKE TO THE PORTER WHO, IN TURN, SPOKE TO JEAN VALJEAN. JEAN VALJEAN MOVED, TAKING COSETTE WITH HIM.

HE HAD NOT LEFT HIS NEW ADDRESS?

NO, MONSIEUR.

MARIUS SEARCHED FOR COSETTE CONTINUALLY.

WHY DID I FOLLOW HER? I WAS SO HAPPY IN SEEING HER ONLY! SHE HAD THE APPEARANCE OF LOVING ME. I WAS A FOOL!

MARIUS LIVED IN A TENEMENT. THE ONLY OTHER OCCUPANTS WERE THE JONDRETTE FAMILY. ONE NIGHT MARIUS CLIMBED UPON A BUREAU AND LOOKED INTO THEIR ROOM.

LET US SEE WHAT THESE PEOPLE ARE, AND TO WHAT THEY ARE REDUCED. PERHAPS I CAN HELP THEM.

MARIUS SAW A FILTHY DEN IN WHICH THE FATHER WAS BUSY WRITING TO BENEVOLENT PERSONS IN ORDER TO RECEIVE THEIR CHARITY. THEN THE ELDER DAUGHTER APPEARED.

THE PHILANTHROPIST IS COMING! I GAVE HIM YOUR LETTER.

WIFE, PUT OUT THE FIRE! QUICK, BREAK A PANE OF GLASS! AH, HOW I HATE THESE CHARITABLE MEN WHO BRING US CLOTHES AND BREAD. I WANT MONEY!

IN A FEW MINUTES THERE WAS A LIGHT RAP AT THE DOOR. THE MAN RUSHED FORWARD AND OPENED IT.

PLEASE COME IN, MY NOBLE BENEFACTOR.

MARIUS SAW A MAN OF MATURE AGE AND A YOUNG GIRL ENTER.

IT IS SHE!

COSETTE STEPPED INTO THE ROOM AND LAID A PACKAGE ON THE TABLE.

MONSIEUR, YOU WILL FIND IN THIS PACKAGE SOME NEW CLOTHES, SOME STOCKINGS AND SOME BLANKETS.

MY BENEFACTOR! BUT TOMORROW, IF I DO NOT PAY THE RENT, WE WILL BE DRIVEN INTO THE STREET. I OWE FOR A YEAR. THAT IS SIXTY FRANCS.

MONSIEUR, I HAVE ONLY THESE FIVE FRANCS WITH ME, BUT I WILL RETURN THIS EVENING AT SIX O'CLOCK WITH SIXTY FRANCS.

AFTER THEY WENT OUT, JONDRETTE WALKED UP AND DOWN WITH RAPID STRIDES.

IT WAS EIGHT YEARS AGO, BUT I RECOGNIZE HIM! AND THAT YOUNG LADY - - IT IS THAT GIRL!

WHAT! THAT LADY? COSETTE?

MY FORTUNE IS MADE. HE WILL COME THIS EVENING. I WILL GET SOME MEN, SOME GOOD ONES. YOU WILL HELP US. HE WILL BE HIS OWN EXECUTOR.

AND IF HE SHOULD NOT BE HIS OWN EXECU-TOR?

WE WILL EXECUTE HIM.

MARIUS GOT DOWN FROM THE BUREAU AS QUIETLY AS HE COULD.

I MUST PUT MY FOOT ON THESE WRETCHES.

HE FOUND A POLICE INSPECTOR AND RELATED HIS ADVENTURE.

TAKE THESE PISTOLS. GO BACK HOME AND WATCH. I WILL BE OUTSIDE. WHEN YOU DEEM IT IS TIME TO STOP THE AFFAIR, FIRE OFF A PISTOL.

BE ASSURED, I WILL.

MARIUS PLACED HIS HAND ON THE LATCH OF THE DOOR TO GO OUT.

BY THE WAY, IF YOU NEED ME BETWEEN NOW AND THEN, COME OR SEND HERE. ASK FOR INSPECTOR JAVERT.

MARIUS RETURNED TO HIS ROOM AND RESUMED HIS PLACE AT HIS OBSERVATORY. WHEN SIX O'CLOCK STRUCK, THE DOOR OF THE JONDRETTE DEN OPENED, AND JEAN VALJEAN WALKED IN.

THIS IS FOR YOUR RENT AND YOUR PRESSING WANTS.

GOD REWARD YOU, MY GENEROUS BENEFACTOR.

A MAN CAME INTO THE ROOM NOISELESSLY. JEAN VALJEAN TURNED.

WHO IS THAT?

A NEIGHBOR. PAY NO ATTENTION TO HIM.

THREE MORE MEN SLIPPED IN.

DO NOT MIND THEM. THEY ARE PEOPLE OF THE HOUSE. BUT THAT IS NOT THE QUESTION! DO YOU KNOW ME?

JONDRETTE LEANED FORWARD LIKE A WILD BEAST JUST ABOUT TO BITE.

MY NAME IS NOT JONDRETTE, MY NAME IS THENARDIER! I AM THE INN KEEPER OF MONTFERMEIL! NOW DO YOU KNOW ME?

NO.

IT WAS YOU WHO CAME TO MY INN EIGHT YEARS AGO AND TOOK FONTINE'S CHILD FROM MY HOUSE. WELL, TRUMPS ARE IN MY HAND TODAY. I MUST HAVE AN IMMENSE AMOUNT OF MONEY, OR I WILL KILL YOU.

JEAN VALJEAN ROSE, AND WITH ONE BOUND WAS AT THE WINDOW. HE WAS HALF OUTSIDE WHEN SIX STRONG HANDS DREW HIM FORCIBLY BACK INTO THE ROOM.

A STRUGGLE COMMENCED. JEAN VALJEAN DISAPPEARED UNDER THE HORRIBLE GROUP OF BANDITS LIKE A WILD BOAR UNDER A HOWLING PACK OF HOUNDS.

THEY SUCCEEDED IN BINDING HIM TO THE BEDPOST. THENARDIER SAT DOWN IN FRONT OF HIM.

I HAVE NOTICED THAT YOU HAVE NOT MADE THE LEAST OUTCRY. I WILL TELL YOU WHY--BECAUSE YOU ARE NO MORE ANXIOUS THAN WE TO SEE POLICE COME. YOU ARE CONCEALING SOMETHING.

NOW WE CAN COME TO AN UNDER-STANDING. I WANT TWO HUNDRED THOU-SAND FRANCS.

DO YOU IMAGINE THAT YOU CAN MAKE ME DO WHAT I DO NOT WISH TO DO?

SUDDENLY JEAN VALJEAN SHOOK OFF HIS BONDS, WHICH HE HAD MANAGED TO CUT WITH A LIT-TLE SAW CONCEALED IN A LARGE COIN.

KILL HIM!

MARIUS' FINGER WAS ON THE TRIGGER OF HIS PISTOL WHEN THE DOOR OPENED AND JAVERT STEPPED INTO THE ROOM.

JEAN VALJEAN TOOK ADVANTAGE OF THE CONFUSION THAT FOLLOWED TO LEAP OUT OF THE WINDOW. JAVERT LOOKED OUT. NOBODY COULD BE SEEN.

THE DEVIL! THAT MUST HAVE BEEN THE BEST ONE!

AFTER JAVERT HAD CARRIED AWAY HIS PRISONERS, MARIUS LEFT THE HOUSE. HE HAD FOR A MOMENT SEEN THE YOUNG GIRL HE LOVED, ONLY TO HAVE HER SWEPT AWAY. THEN ONE DAY HE PASSED AN OVERGROWN GARDEN IN A DESERTED PART OF PARIS AND SAW HER.

SHE TURNED HER HEAD AND ROSE. SHE DREW BACK SLOWLY.

DO NOT BE AFRAID OF ME. DO YOU REMEMBER THE DAY YOU LOOKED UPON ME? IT WAS AT THE LUXEMBOURG. IT IS A LONG TIME NOW. I ADORE YOU.

SHE SANK DOWN. HE CAUGHT HER IN HIS ARMS.

YOU LOVE ME, THEN?

HUSH! YOU KNOW IT!

GRADUALLY THEY BEGAN TO TALK. THEY CONFIDED ALL THAT WAS MOST HIDDEN AND MOST MYSTERIOUS IN THEMSELVES. FINALLY...

MY NAME IS MARIUS. AND YOURS?

MY NAME IS COSETTE.

THEREAFTER, MARIUS CAME EVERY EVENING. JEAN VALJEAN SUSPECTED NOTHING. YET HE FELT DANGERS AROUND HIM. THE POLICE HAD BECOME VERY ACTIVE AND SUSPICIOUS, AND HE HAD SEEN THENARDIER, WHO WAS OUT OF PRISON, PROWLING ABOUT.

WE MUST LEAVE HERE.

WHEN MARIUS CAME THAT NIGHT, HE FOUND COSETTE HAD BEEN WEEPING.

MY FATHER TOLD ME THIS MORNING THAT WE WILL BE GOING AWAY TO ENGLAND.

BUT THIS IS MONSTROUS!

I HAVE AN IDEA I WILL TELL YOU WHERE WE ARE GOING, AND YOU CAN JOIN ME THERE.

BUT IT TAKES MONEY, AND I HAVE NONE.

MARIUS LEFT, INTENT ON GETTING SOME MONEY FROM HIS GRANDFATHER. WHEN HE RETURNED, FORTY-EIGHT HOURS LATER, COSETTE WAS NOT THERE. THE HOUSE WAS AS SILENT AND EMPTY AS A TOMB.

MARIUS WAS MAD WITH GRIEF. HE HAD BUT ONE DESIRE -- TO DIE.

I WILL JOIN MY FRIENDS AT THE BARRICADES.

DURING THE TWO MONTHS OF JOY MARIUS HAD HAD WITH COSETTE, AN INSURRECTION AGAINST THE GOVERNMENT HAD BEEN GATHERING. THAT DAY, IT HAD BROKEN OUT IN OPEN CONFLICT. BARRICADES WERE BEING THROWN UP. MARIUS HASTENED TO ONE DEFENDED BY SOME OF HIS FRIENDS. WHEN HE REACHED IT, THE FIGHTING HAD ALREADY BEGUN.

THE SOLDIERS WILL TAKE THE BARRICADE!

HE FOUND A KEG OF POWDER, GLIDED ALONG THE BARRICADE, PUT THE KEG DOWN, AND SEIZED A TORCH.

BEGONE, OR I'LL BLOW UP THE BARRICADE!

BLOW UP THE BARRICADE! AND YOURSELF, ALSO.

AND MYSELF, ALSO.

HE HELD THE TORCH NEARER TO THE KEG OF POWDER. THE SOLDIERS FLED PELL-MELL, AND THE BARRICADE WAS SAVED.

MARIUS' FRIENDS FLOCKED AROUND HIM.

YOU CAME IN GOOD TIME!

WITHOUT YOU WE WOULD HAVE BEEN DEAD.

ONE HELD A LETTER OUT TO HIM.

THIS CAME FOR YOU AT YOUR LODGING.

MARIUS TOOK IT AND FOUND A CANDLE IN A BASEMENT ROOM.

IT IS FROM COSETTE. TONIGHT, SHE WILL BE AT THE RUE DE L'HOMME ARME, NO. 7.

MARIUS FOUND A PIECE OF PAPER AND WROTE A FEW LINES.

Our marriage is impossible. I am without fortune. I die. I love you.

HE GAVE IT TO A MESSENGER TO TAKE TO COSETTE. THE MESSENGER, HOWEVER, GAVE IT TO JEAN VALJEAN.

WILL YOU GIVE IT TO THE LADY? I MUST GET BACK TO THE BARRICADE IN THE RUE DE LA CHANVRERIE.

JEAN VALJEAN READ THE LETTER. IT WAS CRUSHING EVIDENCE THAT COSETTE, WHOM HE ADORED AS A DAUGHTER, HAD GLIDED FROM HIS HANDS.

IT MUST BE THAT UNKNOWN PROWLER OF THE LUXEMBOURG. WELL, HE IS GOING TO DIE. I HAVE ONLY TO LET THINGS TAKE THEIR COURSE.

BUT WITHIN HIMSELF HE BECAME GLOOMY. ABOUT AN HOUR AFTERWARD, HE WENT OUT IN THE DIRECTION OF THE BARRICADE.

CITIZEN, YOU ARE WELCOME. YOU KNOW THAT WE ARE GOING TO DIE.

IN A BASEMENT ROOM BEHIND THE BARRICADE, JEAN VALJEAN SAW A MAN BOUND TO A POST.

YOU ARE A SPY.

I AM JAVERT, AN OFFICER OF THE GOVERNMENT.

YOU WILL BE SHOT TEN MINUTES BEFORE THE BARRICADE IS TAKEN.

WHY NOT IMMEDIATELY?

FROM THE THRESHOLD, JEAN VALJEAN GAZED AT HIM WITH SINGULAR ATTENTION. JAVERT RAISED HIS EYES.

IT IS VERY NATURAL FOR YOU TO BE HERE.

Each man resumed his post for combat. They did not have long to wait. A piece of artillery appeared.

FIRE!

The whole barricade flashed fire. An avalanche of smoke covered the gun and the soldiers.

But the gunner began to point his cannon at a break in the barricade with the gravity of an astronomer adjusting a telescope.

HEADS DOWN! KEEP CLOSE TO THE WALL!

The discharge took place with the fearful rattle of grapeshot.

WE CANNOT HOLD OUT A QUARTER OF AN HOUR IN THIS STORM OF GRAPE. WE MUST PUT A MATTRESS IN THE BREAK.

The only mattress was outside the barricade. Jean Valjean went out, passed through a storm of balls, picked up the mattress and returned to the barricade.

HE PUT THE MATTRESS IN THE OPENING. THE CANNON VOMITED ITS PACKAGE OF SHOT WITH A ROAR, BUT THE SHOT MISCARRIED UPON THE MATTRESS. THE BARRICADE WAS PRESERVED.

CITIZEN, THE REPUBLIC THANKS YOU.

BUT THE FIRE OF THE SOLDIERS CONTINUED. A SECOND CANNON WAS BROUGHT UP. THEN ANOTHER PLATOON APPEARED. THE END WAS NEAR.

THE LAST MAN TO LEAVE WILL BLOW OUT THE SPY'S BRAINS!

JEAN VALJEAN APPEARED.

I ASK A FAVOR. I WANT TO BLOW OUT THAT MAN'S BRAINS MYSELF.

NO OBJECTION!

JEAN VALJEAN CAUGHT UP A PISTOL. ALMOST AT THE SAME MOMENT THEY HEARD A FLOURISH OF TRUMPETS. THE INSURGENTS SPRANG FORWARD AND WENT OUT.

YOUR HEALTH IS HARDLY BETTER THAN MINE.

When Jean Valjean was alone with Javert, he untied the rope that held the prisoner and led him into a little street.

TAKE YOUR REVENGE.

Jean Valjean cut the remaining cords.

YOU ARE FREE. GO.

Javert stood aghast and motionless. Then he turned and walked off. Jean Valjean fired the pistol in the air.

He re-entered the barricade. Suddenly the drum beat the charge. The attack was a hurricane. There was assault after assault.

In the thick cloud of combat, Jean Valjean did not take his eyes from Marius. When a shot struck Marius, Jean Valjean bounded with the agility of a tiger and carried him away.

THE ATTACK WAS AT THAT INSTANT SO FIERCE THAT NO ONE SAW JEAN DISAPPEAR BEHIND THE CORNER OF A HOUSE AND STOP IN A LITTLE SHELTERED PLACE.

HOW CAN WE ESCAPE THIS MASSACRE?

HE PERCEIVED AN IRON GRATING LAID FLAT AND LEVEL WITH THE GROUND. TO LIFT IT, DESCEND WITH MARIUS ON HIS BACK, AND FIND A FOOTHOLD ON THE FLAGGED SURFACE TEN FEET BELOW THE GROUND, REQUIRED BUT A FEW MOMENTS.

HE FOUND HIMSELF, WITH MARIUS STILL SENSELESS, IN A LONG, UNDERGROUND PASSAGE.

IT IS THE SEWER.

HE RESOLUTELY ENTERED INTO THE DARKNESS. HE WENT FORWARD SEEING NOTHING, KNOWING NOTHING, PLUNGED INTO CHANCE.

SHALL I FIND AN OUTLET? SHALL I FIND IT IN TIME?

HE HAD BEEN WALKING FOR ABOUT HALF AN HOUR, WHEN ALL AT ONCE HE SAW HIS SHADOW BEFORE HIM. IN AMAZEMENT HE TURNED AROUND.

BEHIND HIM FLAMED A SORT OF HORRIBLE STAR. BEHIND THE STAR WERE EIGHT OR TEN BLACK FORMS, STRAIGHT, INDISTINCT, TERRIBLE.

THE POLICE

HE DREW CLOSE TO THE WALL. THE PATROL RESUMED ITS MARCH, LEAVING JEAN VALJEAN BEHIND.

JEAN VALJEAN RESUMED HIS ADVANCE, WHICH BECAME MORE AND MORE LABORIOUS. HE FELT THAT HE WAS ENTERING THE WATER, AND THAT HE HAD UNDER HIS FEET NO LONGER PAVEMENT, BUT MUD.

HE SOON HAD THE MIRE HALF-KNEE DEEP, AND WATER ABOUT HIS KNEES.

HE SANK IN DEEPER AND DEEPER. THE WATER CAME UP TO HIS WAIST, TO HIS ARMPITS. HE NOW HAD ONLY HIS HEAD OUT OF THE WATER, AND HIS ARMS SUPPORTING MARIUS.

HE SANK STILL DEEPER. HE MADE A DESPERATE EFFORT AND THRUST HIS FOOT FORWARD. HIS FOOT STRUCK SOMETHING SOLID.

HE ASCENDED AN INCLINED PLANE AND REACHED THE OTHER SIDE OF THE QUAGMIRE. HE ROSE, ALL DRIPPING WITH SLIME, HIS SOUL FILLED WITH A STRANGE LIGHT.

HE RESUMED HIS ROUTE ONCE MORE. HIS EXHAUSTION WAS GREAT. THEN HE REACHED AN ANGLE OF THE SEWER AND SAW THE LIGHT OF DAY.

AN OUTLET!

HE REACHED THE OUTLET. THE ARCH WAS CLOSED BY A STRONG GRATING HELD BY A STOUT LOCK.

JEAN VALJEAN CLENCHED THE BARS AND SHOOK THEM. THE GRATING DID NOT STIR. HE DROPPED UPON THE PAVEMENT. HIS HEAD SANK BETWEEN HIS KNEES.

THEN A HAND WAS LAID UPON HIS SHOULDER.

GO HALVES?

JEAN VALJEAN THOUGHT HE WAS DREAMING. HE RAISED HIS EYES AND SAW THENARDIER.

WHAT DO YOU MEAN?

YOU HAVEN'T KILLED THAT MAN WITHOUT LOOKING TO SEE WHAT HE HAD IN HIS POCKETS. GIVE ME HALF. I WILL OPEN THE DOOR FOR YOU.

JEAN VALJEAN TURNED OUT HIS POCKET AND DISPLAYED HIS MONEY. THENARDIER TOOK ALL OF IT. THEN HE OPENED THE DOOR.

JEAN VALJEAN FOUND HIMSELF OUTSIDE. SUDDENLY HE FELT AN INDESCRIBABLE UNEASINESS. HE TURNED AROUND.

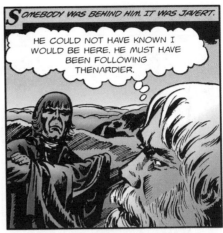

SOMEBODY WAS BEHIND HIM. IT WAS JAVERT.

HE COULD NOT HAVE KNOWN I WOULD BE HERE. HE MUST HAVE BEEN FOLLOWING THENARDIER.

JAVERT'S LOOK WAS TERRIBLE.

WHAT ARE YOU DOING HERE? AND WHO IS THIS MAN?

DISPOSE OF ME AS YOU PLEASE, BUT FIRST HELP ME CARRY HIM HOME.

JEAN VALJEAN SHOWED JAVERT A NOTE ON WHICH MARIUS HAD WRITTEN HIS GRANDFATHER'S ADDRESS. JAVERT CALLED A CARRIAGE, MARIUS WAS LAID ON THE BACK SEAT, AND IT MOVED RAPIDLY OFF.

THE CARRIAGE ARRIVED AT THE HOUSE, AND MARIUS WAS CARRIED IN. JAVERT AND JEAN VALJEAN RETURNED TO THE CARRIAGE.

INSPECTOR JAVERT, GRANT ME ONE THING MORE. LET ME GO HOME A MOMENT. THEN YOU SHALL DO WITH ME WHAT YOU WILL.

VERY WELL.

THEY ARRIVED AT THE STREET WHERE JEAN VALJEAN LIVED. JAVERT DISMISSED THE CARRIAGE.

GO UP. I WILL WAIT HERE FOR YOU.

JEAN VALJEAN MOUNTED THE STAIRS. ON REACHING THE FIRST STORY HE PAUSED AND LOOKED OUT OF THE WINDOW. JAVERT WAS GONE.

JAVERT MADE HIS WAY WITH SLOW STEPS TO THE SEINE, WHERE HE LEANED ON THE PARAPET AND REFLECTED. HE WAS SUFFERING FRIGHTFULLY.

I OWE MY LIFE TO A CONVICT AND I HAVE SET HIM FREE. CAN THERE BE A MYSTERIOUS JUSTICE ACCORDING TO GOD WHICH GOES AGAINST JUSTICE ACCORDING TO MAN?

AUTHORITY WAS DEAD IN JAVERT. HE HAD NO FURTHER REASON FOR EXISTENCE. HE BENT HIS HEAD AND LOOKED AT THE WATER.

THEN HE SPRANG UP ON THE PARAPET, FELL STRAIGHT INTO THE DARKNESS AND DISAPPEARED UNDER THE WATER.

FOUR MONTHS PASSED BEFORE MARIUS WAS OUT OF DANGER. THEN COSETTE CAME TO SEE HIM.

IT IS YOU! HOW HAPPY I AM!

MARIUS HAD ONE PREOCCUPATION -- TO FIND THE MAN WHO HAD BROUGHT HIM TO HIS GRANDFATHER'S HOUSE.

HE MUST HAVE SNATCHED ME OUT OF THE COMBAT AND CARRIED ME FOR MORE THAN FOUR MILES THROUGH THE SEWER.

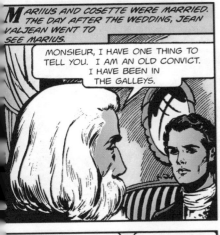

MARIIUS AND COSETTE WERE MARRIED. THE DAY AFTER THE WEDDING, JEAN VALJEAN WENT TO SEE MARIUS.

MONSIEUR, I HAVE ONE THING TO TELL YOU. I AM AN OLD CONVICT. I HAVE BEEN IN THE GALLEYS.

MARUS STOOD AGHAST.

WHY DO YOU TELL ME THIS?

I DO NOT WISH TO BURDEN THE HAPPINESS OF OTHERS WITH MY OWN MISERY. WHAT IF ONE DAY THE POLICE SPRING OUT OF THE SHADOW AND TEAR OFF MY MASK?

I ENTREAT YOU, MONSIEUR, DO NOT TELL THIS TO COSETTE. IT WOULD APPALL HER.

BE CALM. I WILL KEEP YOUR SECRET.

NOW THAT YOU KNOW THIS, I WILL TRY TO SEE COSETTE AS SELDOM AS POSSIBLE.

I THINK THAT WOULD BE BEST.

JEAN VALJEAN'S CONFESSION LEFT MARIUS COMPLETELY UNHINGED. HE FELT A CERTAIN HORROR FOR THE FORMER CONVICT.

JEAN VALJEAN FELT IT. SOON HE DID NOT VISIT COSETTE AT ALL. HE BECAME VERY ILL.

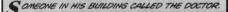

SOMEONE IN HIS BUILDING CALLED THE DOCTOR.

WHAT IS THE MATTER WITH HIM?

HE IS A MAN, IT WOULD APPEAR, WHO HAS LOST SOME DEAR FRIEND. PEOPLE DIE OF THAT.

THEN ONE DAY MARIUS HAD A CALLER. IT WAS THENARDIER.

MONSIEUR, A MAN HAS GLIDED INTO YOUR FAMILY UNDER A FALSE NAME. HE IS JEAN VALJEAN, AN OLD CONVICT. I HAVE AN EXTRAORDINARY SECRET ABOUT HIM. IT IS FOR SALE.

MARIUS THREW HIM A BANK NOTE.

ABOUT A YEAR AGO, ON THE DAY OF THE UPRISING, I WAS IN THE SEWER OF PARIS. THERE I SAW JEAN VALJEAN CARRYING ON HIS SHOULDERS THE CORPSE OF SOMEONE HE HAD ASSASSINATED.

MARIUS ROSE UP, QUIVERING.

YOU ARE A WRETCH! YOU CAME TO ACCUSE THIS MAN, BUT YOU HAVE JUSTIFIED HIM. I WAS THE MAN UPON HIS BACK! IT WAS HE WHO SAVED MY LIFE!

MARIUS AND COSETTE HASTENED TO JEAN VALJEAN'S ROOM.

YOU ARE HERE? I THOUGHT I WOULD NEVER SEE YOU AGAIN. OH, I WAS VERY MISERABLE.

WE ARE GOING TO TAKE YOU BACK WITH US. WE WILL HAVE BUT ONE THOUGHT HENCEFORTH-- YOUR HAPPINESS.

IT WOULD BE CHARMING. ONLY, I SHALL DIE IN A FEW MINUTES.

COME CLOSER, BOTH OF YOU. I LOVE YOU DEARLY. OH! IT IS GOOD TO DIE SO!

COSETTE AND MARIUS FELL ON THEIR KNEES, EACH GRASPING ONE OF JEAN VALJEAN'S HANDS. THEY COVERED THIS HANDS WITH KISSES. HE WAS DEAD.

THE END

LES MISERABLES
VICTOR HUGO

The Author

Les Misérables took nearly twenty years to write. During that time Victor Hugo's life took on some of the adventurous aspects of some of his characters, for he was deeply, passionately devoted to social causes— so much so that just as his career and success had brought him to the top of French literary society, he was forced into exile for twenty years.

Hugo was born in 1802—at the end of the French Revolution. He was two years old when his family first moved to Paris, which became his heart's home. His childhood years were spent moving about with his father, then returning to Paris, so he experienced more than most what life was like during the second half of the Revolution.

Very early Hugo showed interest in writing, and though for a time he studied law, before he turned twenty he founded a literary magazine. He married young, and for a time wrote mainly verse and plays. It was through these plays that he enjoyed his first successes.

He gained even more success when his novel *The Hunchback of Notre Dame* was published in 1831.

Through his young manhood Hugo's political ideas changed as often as his father's had (his father, an army officer, had sworn loyalty to the Convention, to Napoleon, and to the Restoration in their turns) but throughout these shifts in allegiance, there was one constant: he was always a Romantic. He socialized with other Romantic writers, and all his life his works displayed the passions

Isn't It Romantic?

When you speak of Victor Hugo as a Romantic, you're not talking about his love life.... The Romantic Movement in art and literature lasted from about 1750 to 1870, and was a reaction to the Enlightenment movement of the 18th century, when reason, scientific inquiry and logic ruled. The Romantics believed in passion, in the value of their own feelings and subjective experience, in imagination rather than reason, emotion over logic. If form (in literature, in painting, even in music) got in the way of passion and spontaneity, then form took a back seat. The sharp reader will find all the great Romantic themes in *Les Misérables*: freedom and the importance of the human spirit in the face of political repression; the beauty and power of nature; the power of the supernatural; the appeal of the picturesque and exotic; the nobility of the common man. Politically and emotionally, Victor Hugo was one of the great Romantics, but others include philosophers such as Jean Jacques Rousseau, poets like Wordsworth, Coleridge, Schiller, Blake and Shelley, novelists like Dostoyevsky, Nathaniel Hawthorne, Sir Walter Scott, and composers like Beethoven, Schubert, Berlioz and Brahms.

of his romantic ideals.

In 1837 Victor Hugo was awarded the *Legion d'Honneur*. In 1841 he was elected to the *Academie Francaise*, an honor every French writer aspired to, and in 1845 he was made a peer of France, which made him a noble for life—and meant he was automatically a member of the government's Upper House. This was, unfortunately, two years after the single worst event of his life, the accidental drowning of his beloved daughter Leopoldine, in 1843.

After the Revolution of 1848 (which Hugo discusses in *Les Misérables* during the section on insurrections, *despite* the fact that the events of his novel end in 1832!), he became a member of the Constituent Assembly of the new Republic—but when Louis Napoleon took over and established the Second Empire in 1851, Hugo was utterly disgusted and did nothing to hide his opinions. An ardent Republican, he was subsequently forced to leave France.

For nearly twenty years he lived in the Channel Islands, where he did most of his writing. It was here that he finished the book many consider his masterpiece, *Les Misérables*. It gained him world renown.

He returned to Paris in 1870, after the start of the Third Republic, and became involved in the stirring, sometimes violent, politics of the time.

The '70s were a troubled decade for Hugo. He continued to write, but he was tired, and depressed by the deaths of two more of his children and the mental illness of a third. He suffered severe illness in 1878, but lived on for almost a decade. Upon his death in 1885, Hugo was given a national funeral, and lies buried in the Panthéon.

How would you like to wake up one morning and find out that the calendar had been revised by the government, and instead of calling the day (for example) December 4th 1993, you had to say Frumaire 14, Year Two—or else you could go to prison?

—If you forgot to call various adults "Citizen" instead of "Mr." or "Mrs." or—especially—"Lord" and "Lady," you could wind up in a cart on the way to the guillotine to have your head chopped off?

—Despite everyone talking about how people were now completely free of old rules, if you worshipped in the religious faith of your choice, you would go to jail?

These are things that really happened, not in 1993, but in 1793—during the portion of the French Revolution often called the Reign of Terror.

Revolution and Change

The French Revolution's official beginning is listed as July 14, 1789, when a crowd of people from the city of Paris stormed the Bastille—the ancient, much-feared prison where the Kings of France traditionally sent their enemies, often without any kind of trial—and freed the prisoners there. Former kings had filled that prison with people who usually never reappeared. The last king, Louis XVI, ironically enough, was not even remotely as high-handed with summary justice as his forefathers had been. In fact he was a shy, sensitive man, who felt deeply for the plight of his people but didn't know how to solve the problems he'd inherited along with his throne. His ambivalence and indecision, seen by citizens of high and low degree alike as weakness, would cost him his life.

On July 14th, 1789, the Bastille only had fourteen prisoners (two of whom had gone crazy in the years they'd been stuck in a cell and forgotten), but it was an important symbol. The people, who had become increasingly dissatisfied with the governments led by kings and nobles, showed that they were no longer afraid of the aristocrats—no matter how rich and powerful they were.

Troubles and unrest had been going on long before 1789. After what we call the French Revolution officially ended with the fall of Napoleon Bonaparte and the restoration of King Louis XVIII in 1815, there were three more 'official' revolutions during the 1800s—in 1830, 1848, and 1870—and many more uprisings. Victor Hugo's great novel *Les Misérables* begins around the time the French Revolution has ended, and takes the reader up through an uprising in 1832.

THE BISHOP LEFT HIS GUEST BEFORE A CLEAN, WHITE BED.

YOU LODGE ME IN YOUR HOUSE, AS NEAR TO YOU AS THIS! WHO TELLS YOU THAT I AM NOT A MURDERER!

GOD WILL TAKE CARE OF THAT.

Hugo doesn't tell the story of kings, or generals, or of the leaders of the Reign of Terror like Marat and Robespierre. His novel concerns the ordinary people whose lives were changed by the decisions made by these leaders. Some of them—like Marius, and Jean Valjean—become leaders themselves, however briefly. Some are not leaders, but performed heroic deeds. The delightful street kid, Gavroche, stands on the ramparts during that last uprising and dances about making fun of the soldiers who are shooting at him. There is the quiet, everyday heroism of Monseigneur Bienvenu, the elderly priest who gives Jean Valjean his first taste of trust and faith, and thus makes it possible for the hardened criminal to become an honest man. Others become villains, like Thenardier. Still others are not destined for heroism or villainy, but try to make lives for themselves despite the changes about them, like Cosette and Eponine, the Thenardiers' eldest daughter.

These changes were not just political. Hugo shows, in fact, how ordinary people often ignored the doings of the great and mighty, just as today many

JEAN VALJEAN WAS NOT A MURDERER. HE HAD BEEN A PRUNER AT FAVEROLLES, THE SOLE SUPPORT OF HIS WIDOWED SISTER AND HER SEVEN CHILDREN. ONE YEAR THERE WAS A VERY SEVERE WINTER. JEAN HAD NO WORK, THE FAMILY HAD NO BREAD.

WHAT SHALL WE DO?

people ignore what's going on in Washington and keep themselves busy with work, play, and their own family and friends.

For over a thousand years life in France had changed with glacial slowness. For the peasantry, it hadn't changed much at all since the days when kings and nobles went to battle to protect them against marauding Goths, Huns, Vikings, and various other armed brigands—both lawful and unlawful. In return, the peasants worked the fields and raised food. In theory this was a good trade, but in practice the combatants too often trampled the crops the peasants had worked over—yet

the nobles still demanded their due at the yearly rent time. And, since they had the swords, they could enforce their demands with punishment—and death. A peasant whose lord failed to protect him (or whose men had gone on the rampage and robbed him and burned his farm) had no one to enforce his rights. If there was anything (or anyone) left, he could pack up and hit the road—more often than not as a beggar. Increasingly over the years, peasants whose lands had been ruined by war, famine, bad weather, or pests, moved to the cities seeking work. When—as usually happened—there was no work, they still needed food and shelter, so they turned to crime. Once-honest people were driven by hunger and fear into stealing food or shelter—people like Jean Valjean.

The changes during the French Revolution were drastic, and sometimes followed one another so quickly that people had a hard time adjusting. Nowadays kids know what the Internet is, and usually learn something about computers before they leave elementary school. Most of their parents grew up in homes where there was no computer. Their grandparents can remember life before television, and there are people alive today who can talk about what life was like before radio, cars, airplanes—even telephones.

These are only technological changes. Think about some of the other changes and transformative events—events that changed our outlooks, our ways of doing things—in this century alone: war, the Great Depression, changes in governments and ideologies. Look at the Amendments to the Constitution made during the 20th Century. Women were not able to vote until the 19th Amendment was ratified, in 1920. A year before that, the 18th Amendment forbade the manufacture or sale of alcohol in this country—this Amendment, which was a complete disaster, was repealed in 1933. None of these changes were made without passionate speeches from people on both sides, and sometimes even riots.

During the French Revolution, each new government tried to rewrite the rules

Some Background Details

In reading a book set elsewhere and else-when, it's sometimes useful to have a few bits of special knowledge.

Francs and *sous*: French money during this period was a mixture of coins from various royal and revolutionary governments, each with differing values which changed as the economic situation changed. Think of sous as small change—approximately a nickel—and francs as approximately a dollar.

Galleys. Sail ships propelled by oars in order to increase speed, or provide speed when there is little wind. Male convicts were sentenced to long years in the galleys. They spent their time chained to benches, living and sleeping in the same spot. Life was rough, food scant, and punishments severe. Great numbers of galley-convicts died before their sentences could be served. Afterward they were required to carry a passport stating that they were convicts, so that honest people would be warned wherever they went.

Gendarmerie: in those days, local authorities often clashed with the jurisdictions of royal and ecclesiastical authorities. The Revolution made things even more complicated. Think of the gendarmes as local people, who might or might not have had training in arms, and who functioned mostly on a volunteer basis.

for living with the admirable goal of redressing ancient inequalities. There were good changes made: feudalism was ended, and Declaration of Rights was issued in 1789. There were also terrible changes, such as the legalized terror instigated by the Committee of Public Safety, which guaranteed that those in power could control the rest of the revolutionaries. Such overnight solutions to age-old problems simply didn't work; even less effective was vengeance: in some provinces, after the peasants spent the spring and summer burning down the nobles' castles, destroying their property, and guillotining their families and servants, they returned to their own lands to find that no one had tended the crops in the meantime. This meant they faced oncoming winter with no food stored; the nobles were gone, but they were even worse off than they'd been before.

In revolutionary France, people began to get used to the fact that the basic rules for living might change any day. It was difficult to trust the laws and authorities, for not only did they not keep their promises to maintain peace and promote prosperity—they might be replaced at any time by a brand-new group of leaders who would repeal all the recent laws and issue new ones. At the end of the Revolution, the

THE MAN TOOK UP HIS STICK AND KNAPSACK, AND WENT OFF. HE TRIED SEVERAL HOUSES AND WAS TURNED AWAY. NIGHT CAME ON. EXHAUSTED, HE LAY DOWN ON A STONE BENCH.

tragedy was that the basic problems still existed: the cities and countryside were still filled with huge numbers of poverty-stricken, desperate people whose only choices were crime or death. Exhausted, disillusioned, the people at first welcomed the kings back, for at least that was an evil they'd been used to. The evils of the years of revolution had benefited no one, even the leaders: most of them had suffered exile or violent deaths.

But the return of the old ways did not completely wipe out the Revolutionary changes, as the novel shows. Even the simplest people remembered that they had once gotten rid of a king. If need be, they could do it again.

The book is divided into five parts, and each of those into smaller books, which are again divided into chapters. The first three parts are named for characters with whom Jean Valjean comes into contact: "Fantine," "Cosette," and "Marius." Part Four parallels the story of Marius and the story of Jean Valjean, with Cosette as the link: "The Idyll in the Rue Plumet and the Epic of the Rue Saint-Denis." The fifth part is called "Jean Valjean," as all the story links lead back to the man whose misadventures began when he stole a loaf of bread in order to feed his starving family.

The main story in the book *Les Misérables* is, of course, the life of Jean Valjean. But that's not the only story; his is more like the trunk of a great, spreading tree. All the people with whom he comes into contact are like the branches of the tree. The reader is introduced to this or that person first, just as when you spy an oak tree, you look at the foliage—but then your eye is drawn down all the twists and turns of the branch to the trunk. Hugo's novel introduces the reader to a great many memorable characters, but they always lead back to events in the life of Jean Valjean.

One way to look at *Les Misérables*—the way we're going to look at the novel—is by considering themes and images of light and darkness.

Les MISERABLES
VICTOR HUGO

THE UNFORTUNATE AND THE INFAMOUS ARE ASSOCIATED IN THE WORDS, LES MISERABLES. THERE WERE MANY SUCH PEOPLE IN FRANCE IN 1815. ONE OF THEM WAS JEAN VALJEAN.

"The Noxious Poor"

It's hard to provide an exact translation of the French word *misérables*. It's not just "miserable people" or "wretches", though misery is certainly implied. Hugo's *misérables* are the utter outcasts, the people rejected by society, people with nowhere to sleep, no food, no money, often no clothes but what they can pick out of the trash—or steal off a dead body. He usually shows such people in the night, for that is when they can creep abroad and steal what they have been denied the chance to earn honestly.

"Sea and Shadow"

It is in darkness that most of the dramatic events of this book take place. Take a glance back through the Classics Illustrated adaptation:

•Jean Valjean arrives in the town during the evening, and it's at night that he is directed to the home of Monseigneur Bienvenu. It is of course the same night that he steals the silver and takes off.

•When we look back at Jean Valjean's life, it is at night that he first turned thief and tried to steal a loaf of bread to feed his sister's family.

•Fantine stays in a dark attic after she loses her job, and it's at night when she gets into the fight that almost leads to her being thrown in jail.

•It is at night that Jean Valjean arrives to stop the trial—and conviction—of an innocent man. And it is that same night that poor Fantine dies.

•It is later Christmas Night when Jean Valjean finds Fantine's daughter, Cosette, and rescues her from the Thenardiers. They reach Paris at night and find a place to hide. And it is at night that Jean Valjean realizes that Javert has discovered them.

•The chase through the Paris streets is at night.

•It's at night that Marius discovers who his neighbors are—and what evil they are planning to the man who is the "father" of the girl he loves.

•Again, it is at night that the next great crisis happens in Marius's life—he returns to claim Cosette, discovers her gone, and goes to join the barricade at Rue de la Chanvrerie.

WIFE, PUT OUT THE FIRE! QUICK, BREAK A PANE OF GLASS! AH, HOW I HATE THESE CHARITABLE MEN WHO BRING US CLOTHES AND BREAD. I WANT MONEY!

•It is the next night that brings Jean Valjean, after intercepting Marius's note to Cosette. That night sees the defeat of the insurgents, the terrible trip through the sewers, and Javert's suicide.

Many more events in the novel take place in the hours of darkness: Thenardier's "rescue" of Marius's father, and Fantine's encounters with Marius, and most of Gavroche's adventures. Hugo stages many important events inside dark houses (Fantine's sufferings, and the convent life). Cosette's most terrifying moment is at night; Marius goes to see his grandfather at night, and through misunderstanding, they reject each other without meaning to. The prison break is of course at night.

Thenardier's reappearance into Marius's life and Jean Valjean's death all take place in a night.

"What to Do in a Bottomless Pit Except Talk?"

The use of darkness as a symbol for the underworld of the poor, the criminal and the politically "different" is pretty literal. The modern reader has to remember that this story takes place long before the discovery of electricity. The only way to hold back the darkness was with fire, which casts a weak, uneven glow. The very poor could not afford the luxury of candles, not when they couldn't get anything to eat or to keep themselves warm. They went to sleep when the sun set—even though it might set at four o'clock during winter months! That is, honest folk went to bed then. As Hugo shows, the setting of the sun was the signal for Paris's vast underworld to be up and stirring.

In *Les Misérables* Hugo works hard to show the life of the poor and outcast in realistic detail, which means showing how much of life was lived in shadows and cold and gloom.

But the darkness also serves as a symbol for the darkness inside human beings. It is this darkness that Hugo explores extensively, and with just as realistic an eye for detail (probably more!), through the events of this novel.

The darkness Hugo attacks most passionately is ignorance. "The greatest enemy to civilization is ignorance," Hugo says at one point in his book, and again, much later, he comes at it from the opposite side, saying, "The greatest enemy to civilization is darkness." In that chapter he talks about how the criminal life of Paris comes alive as soon as the sun goes down, but he essentially means the same thing. For he goes on to illustrate the lives of the criminals who grew up wretched, poor, and uneducated, and who—if they survive childhood, which too many didn't—often turned into hardened predators.

In the Classics Illustrated adaptation we get just a glimpse of some of these characters. In the book, Hugo describes them in vivid, fascinating asides—he even adds a chapter about the secret slang and codes of thieves. When Eponine, the Thenardiers' oldest daughter, says "It's a biscuit" to a prisoner whom she visits in jail, that person passes on to the others in his gang that the house Eponine checked out isn't going to be a safe hideout.

Good and bad, these underworld characters come to life in the novel. I mentioned Gavroche before. Even more delightful to read about than Charles Dickens's famed Artful Dodger in *Oliver Twist*, Gavroche is vividly described, from his cast-away clothing (he doesn't care if it belonged to man or woman) to his taste for sneaking into the grand Parisian theatres to watch plays. Even at the end, when the uprising is not far away, and he has to deliver a letter to Jean Valjean, he can't resist picking up stones and knocking out the street lamps with an expert flick of the wrist, just to scare the populace hiding in trembling fear in the houses up and down the street. "Now you've got your nightcap on," he says irrepressibly—but what he really means is that now they are all equal in darkness.

"The Gallantry of Absolute Obedience"

Hugo doesn't just show us the criminals. He also gives us a glimpse into the lives of those who choose to live in poverty and darkness—those belonging to the religious communities, a very important element of French culture of the time. The book opens with a leisurely look at the life of the saintly Monseigneur Bienvenu, the priest who was

THE NEXT DAY, THREE GENDARMES BROUGHT JEAN VALJEAN BACK TO THE BISHOP'S HOUSE.

AH, THERE YOU ARE! I AM GLAD TO SEE YOU. I GAVE YOU THE CANDLESTICKS, ALSO; WHY DID YOU NOT TAKE THEM ALONG WITH YOUR PLATES?

born a minor noble, but who chose priesthood. He gives away everything he owns except his fine dishes and his silver candelabra, beautiful objects which please his aesthetic sense when he sits down each evening to his scanty meal. But even the candlesticks are given away to Jean Valjean, who at this point appears to be a hardened criminal. Monseigneur sees only a desperate man, and when he gives the candlesticks to Valjean, he says, "With these I withdraw your soul from dark thoughts and give it to God." The old priest takes this action without regret. Monseigneur

Bienvenu is content to hold back the darkness with a single poor candle, for he is not afraid of night and its mysteries: his faith is an inner light.

Later on in the story, as the Classics Illustrated adaptation shows, Jean Valjean and Cosette are sheltered in a convent after a harrowing chase by Javert and his men through the wintry streets of Paris. In the book, Hugo takes the time to show what life in a convent was like for the girls schooled at the Benedictine-Bernardine retreat at Petit-Picpus. Hugo shows the human aspects of the life, the little, fascinating details. For example, if a girl knocked at a door she had to say, "Praise and worship to the Holy Sacrament of the altar," and the one inside would respond, "For ever." This became such habit that some of the girls, even after they'd left the convent school and married, would automatically mutter "For ever!" if someone knocked at their door. Silence was supposed to rule, so many of the events of the day would be des-

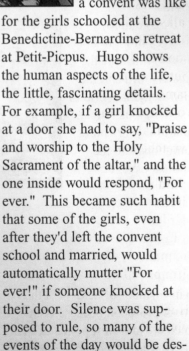

ignated by bells. The girls used the bell tolls as a kind of code—going to class was referred to as "going to six-five"; an emergency was referred to as a "nineteen." Hugo also describes the horrors that were sometimes perpetrated against defenseless girls by unscrupulous authorities in the name of religion—like being locked away in solitary confinement in a tiny cell underground, ostensibly to pray your life out, but probably to die in utter madness and desolation.

"Disorder the Upholder of Order"

Hugo employs images of night not just to illustrate the underworld and the self-denying world of the religious retreat, but to explore human emotions and the human psyche.

After the tremendously exciting battle at the barricade of the Rue de Chanvrerie, Jean Valjean carries Marius on his back through the disgusting and terrifying sewers of Paris. This symbol of descent is the more profound because both men are at lowest points of their lives. Marius, on the verge of death, thinks himself separated from Cosette; Jean Valjean, whose only joy in life is his adopted daughter Cosette, believes himself about to lose her for ever. Each man loves Cosette, so desperately he sees the other as an enemy—and each thinks he has lost her, and thus is ready to give up his life. They do not communicate their fears, and this last ignorance—of each other— nearly destroys these gallant people at the end. After all the great events, it is finally Thenardier's ill-intentioned interference that brings them all together again, in understanding and love, when it is almost too late.

HE ASCENDED AN INCLINED PLANE AND REACHED THE OTHER SIDE OF THE QUAGMIRE. HE ROSE, ALL DRIPPING WITH SLIME, HIS SOUL FILLED WITH A STRANGE LIGHT.

DURING THE TWO MONTHS OF JOY MARIUS HAD HAD WITH COSETTE, AN INSURRECTION AGAINST THE GOVERNMENT HAD BEEN GATHERING. THAT DAY, IT HAD BROKEN OUT IN OPEN CONFLICT. BARRICADES WERE BEING THROWN UP. MARIUS HASTENED TO ONE DEFENDED BY SOME OF HIS FRIENDS. WHEN HE REACHED IT, THE FIGHTING HAD ALREADY BEGUN.

THE SOLDIERS WILL TAKE THE BARRICADE!

"Hunt in Darkness"

The last kind of inner dark that Hugo explores is that of unreasoning law—embodied in the person of Javert, the police sergeant who pursues Jean

Valjean through most of the book. Javert is yet another man born into ignorance and poverty, abandoned at an early age by abusive parents who were themselves victims of poverty. He chose the law as a way to fight against the chaos of the criminal world, but in Javert justice is the equivalent of vengeance. He obeys the letter of the law. The spirit of the law—protection of citizens' rights—is nothing Javert concerns himself with. The enlightenment that rehabilitation brings, that mercy and faith cast, is denied by Javert until the very end, and, unable to face it even then, he flings himself off a bridge into darkness, and drowns in the river. Hugo comes back to this theme several times during the book, showing that laws alone will not fix the problems besetting society; at the very beginning, the gentle Monseigneur Bienvenu walks through a city and chances on a guillotine, terrifying symbol of the law. He never walks that way again; for him, governmental law is a puzzle he cannot solve, and he trusts only to the laws of God.

JAVERT MADE HIS WAY WITH SLOW STEPS TO THE SEINE. WHERE HE LEANED ON THE PARAPET AND REFLECTED. HE WAS SUFFERING FRIGHTFULLY.

I OWE MY LIFE TO A CONVICT AND I HAVE SET HIM FREE. CAN THERE BE A MYSTERIOUS JUSTICE ACCORDING TO GOD WHICH GOES AGAINST JUSTICE ACCORDING TO MAN?

"Light and More Light"

A priest can withdraw from the world, but many times the people—fathers, brothers, those with families to provide for and protect—don't have that choice. Furious because they are forced to obey laws that do not protect them or enable them to earn an honest living, they resort to riot. When Marius joins the insurgents behind the barricade at the Rue de la Chanvrerie, Hugo takes the time to move into the minds and hearts of the rioters. He shows how they could come to gamble their lives on desperate, violent action—and then he shows that their families will suffer the more for their deaths. When the main provider is gone, the family is cast into the outer darkness.

At the end of the novel, the reader has raced along, eager to find out what happens to the characters through the exciting events. The characters are so alive, and their adventures so vivid, one is scarcely aware that one has read one of the greatest pieces of social criticism ever written. But when one closes the book and has time to reflect, one can see that Hugo has shown that governments that enforce their power through violence and coercion are no more effective than revolutionaries who kill and destroy, then use further violence to keep their power. Hugo tries to show, through the lives of ordinary people, that the true way to peace and prosperity is through the light of education, choice, and faith.

"The End of A Day's Journey"

How realistic is *Les Misérables*? Hugo not only draws on his own memories and experiences in order to tell his story; it is clear from the text that he trod the streets of Paris himself, describing in detail what the buildings looked before and during the Revolution, and what took their place afterward. He pored over maps, newspapers, and police reports in order to give as realistic a detail as he could; time and again he drops out of the fictional narrative to advise the reader to check the map of the period, or the newspaper of this or that date, or the police report, there to find a similar story belonging to a real human being.

Unfortunately, as careful modern scholars have discovered, newspapers and police reports in the 1800s were much more prone to factual error—intentional as well as inadvertent—than they are now. And there were times when Hugo's memory was wrong about where this street lay, or when that building was torn down.

The dispassionate historian, asked, "How realistic is this novel?" would probably say, "Not very." But that's why great literature endures—it transcends factual details (which no one remembers correctly anyway) to show a greater truth about human nature. Hugo's real genius lay with psychological realism. We can believe in his characters, we can empathize with them—or when we can't empathize, we can at least understand what made them behave the way they do. Hugo's characters act like real people. We know there never was a Jean Valjean or a Cosette or a Marius, but if we read biographies of the time we discover hundreds of people who could have been any of these characters, whose lives were wrenched in the same ways by war and revolution and harsh laws; who thought, and felt, and laughed, and loved, lived and died, just as these characters did. And such was Hugo's skill as a writer, he makes us see them, suffer with them, laugh with them, our hearts racing when they are in danger. When the book is over, they seem for a time as real as the people around us.

No less real than the people is Hugo's central concern, to push back the darkness of ignorance, to benefit civilization. Despite the hundred-fifty years between Hugo's time and ours, we still face many of the same problems: greed, violence, ugly and unsafe tenements, homeless people; the rich and powerful exploiting the poor and weak.

Let me quote a part of the conversation between the old Revolutionary and the old priest during the early chapters. The Revolutionary is defending his actions, for he says his motivation was to better humankind. The priest points out that the Reign of Terror did not benefit anyone.

"Ah, 1793! I thought we would come to that. The clouds had been gathering for fifteen hundred years and at last the storm broke. What you are condemning is a thunderclap."

The priest replies: "The judge speaks in the name of justice. The priest speaks in the name of pity, which is only a higher form of justice. A thunderclap must not be mistaken."

"Man is ruled by a tyrant whose name is Ignorance, and that is the tyrant I sought to overthrow. We should be ruled by knowledge."

"And by conscience," says the priest.

And the Revolutionary joins their two aims together like this: "They are the same thing. Conscience is the amount of inner knowledge that we possess."

Read this novel. Read other great novels. Great literature enriches your experience, and it is through experience and knowledge that we come to wisdom. Perhaps it will be your generation that achieves Hugo's goal: peace and prosperity for every human being born under the sun.

Study Questions

•Read about the reigns of Louis XVI and Marie Antoinette. Was the Revolution their fault? Do you think they could have stopped it?

•What do you think is the moment that turns Jean Valjean from a criminal to a reformed life? Why does he repeatedly jeopardize his new life—in which he does good for many people? Does Hugo seem to be saying that Valjean cannot outrun his past?

•Who were the Romantics, and what were their ideals?

•It may seem melodramatic to us that Marius is ready to die when he believes he can't marry Cosette. What would you have told him?

•How do the rebellious students of *Les Misérables* compare with students of our time? With students of the late 1960s?

•Look up the Bastille, and prison life during its years.

•Why does Javert kill himself? Do you have an idea (or ideal) in your life that you would consider dying for?

•If (as Hugo suggests) the insurgents' deaths at the barricades won't change anything—and indeed, may leave their families worse off than before—are they heroes? Or fools?

About the Essayist:

Sherwood Smith holds an MA from UC Santa Barbara; she is the author of numerous adult and young adult fantasy and science fiction books, including *Wren's War* (HBJ '95), and *Rifter's Covenant* (Tor '95). Ms. Smith teaches at Carden Conservatory.